He could hang out with Jerble and go fishing. If he could only find a way to fish, swim and hang out with Jerble then life or at least Derble's life would be perfect.

Today Derble decided to go fishing at the pond
past the hill. He usually goes fishing at the
Stream or when he goes swimming
everymorning but he wanted
to try Some place new.

Next to swimming and hanging out with his cousin Jerble,
Derble's most favorite thing to do was to go fishing.
He could not remember when he didn't really
look forward to going.

He liked fishing so much, that when he was younger,
he even taught Jerble how to fish. Which
made fishing that much more fun.

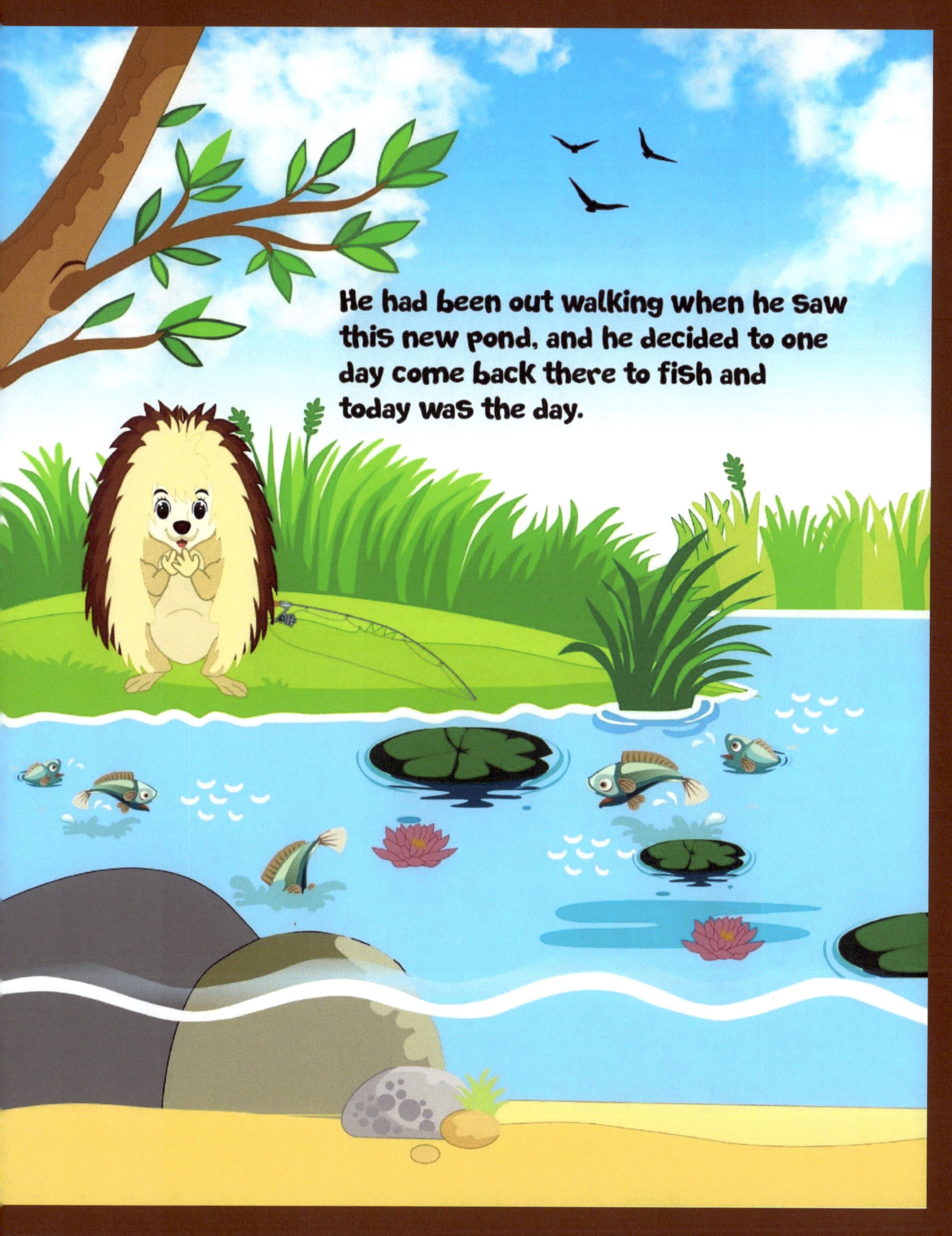
He had been out walking when he saw
this new pond, and he decided to one
day come back there to fish and
today was the day.

So he went swimming in the morning as he always does. Then he went home and had his lunch. He had already caught some worms the night before, so after lunch, it was time to go.

Off he headed, to the pond past the hill. It would take a little while to get there, but Derble was sure that it would be well worth it.

When Derble finaly got to the top of
the hill, he stopped to look around
and see where the best spot
to fish would be.

The pond was really something. When Derble first found it, he didn't notice how wonderful a pond it was, but he did now. It was just the right size, it was just the right color.

It was sitting at the bottom of the hill,
which meant that it wouldn't be too
windy. there were trees around it,
and fish loved to swim in the shade
of trees and Derble knew it.

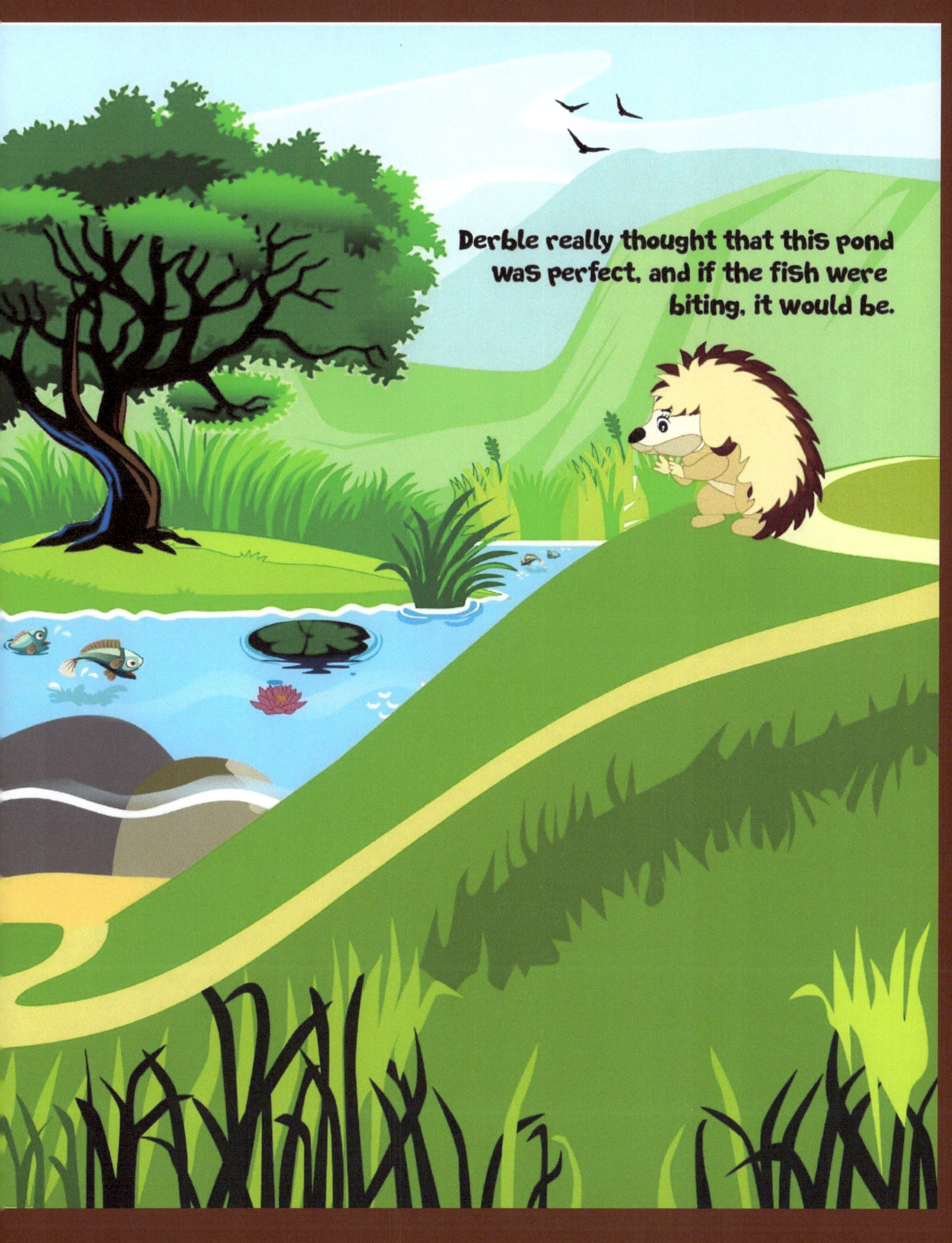

Derble really thought that this pond was perfect, and if the fish were biting, it would be.

Derble decided to fish next to an
old willow tree whose branches
were hanging almost in
the water.

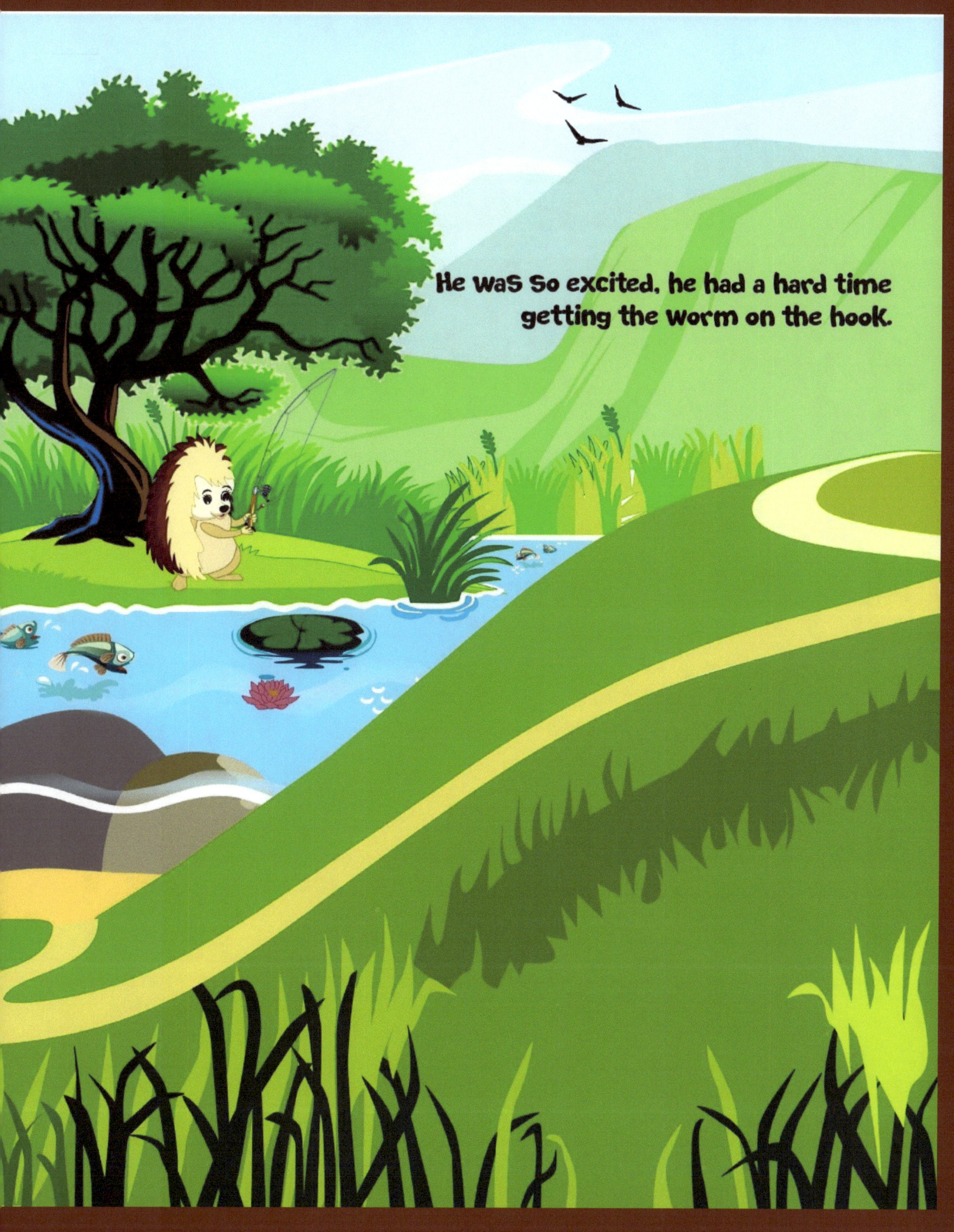

He was so excited, he had a hard time getting the worm on the hook.

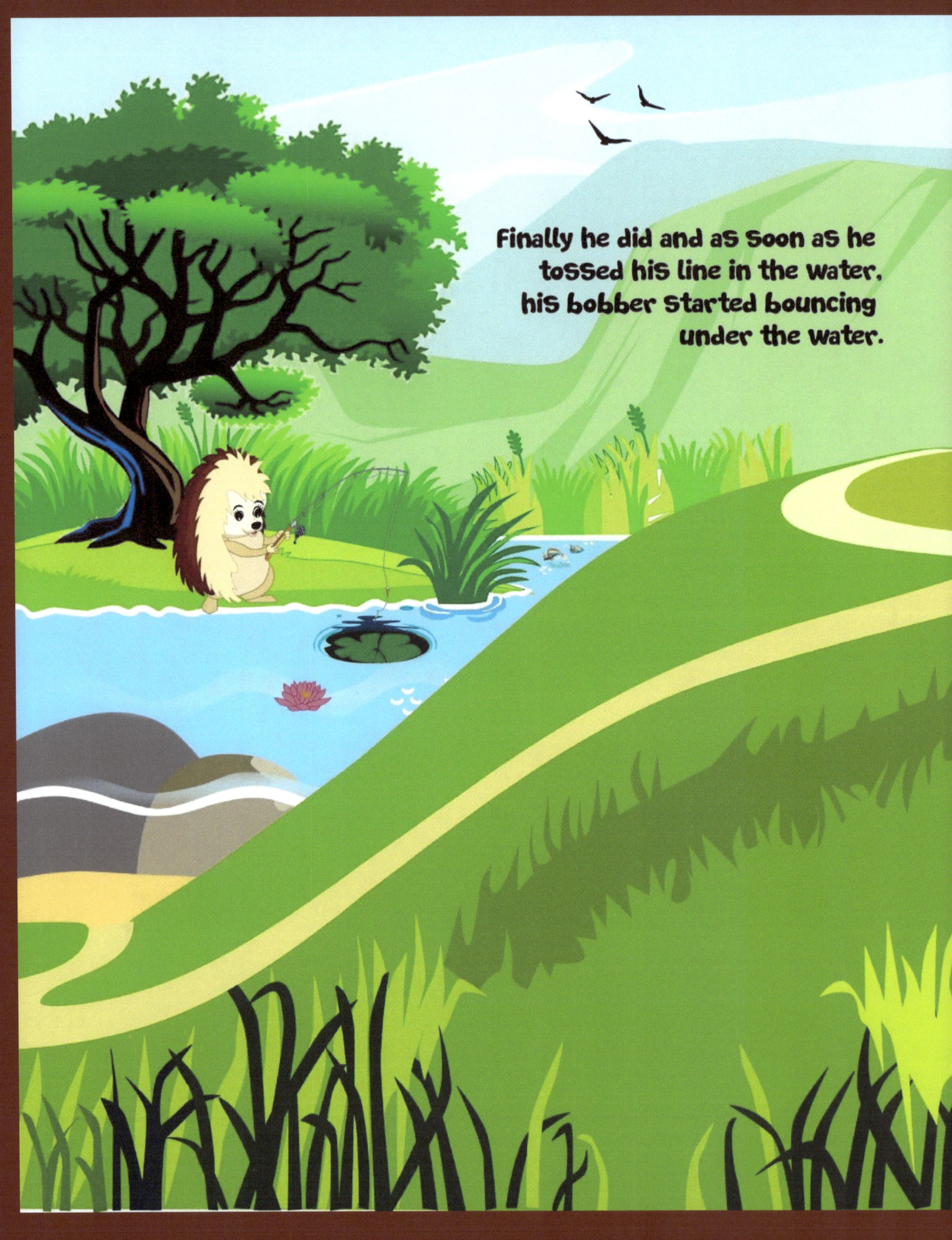

Finally he did and as soon as he tossed his line in the water, his bobber started bouncing under the water.

This usualy means that a fish has taken his worm and that Derble has caught a fish.

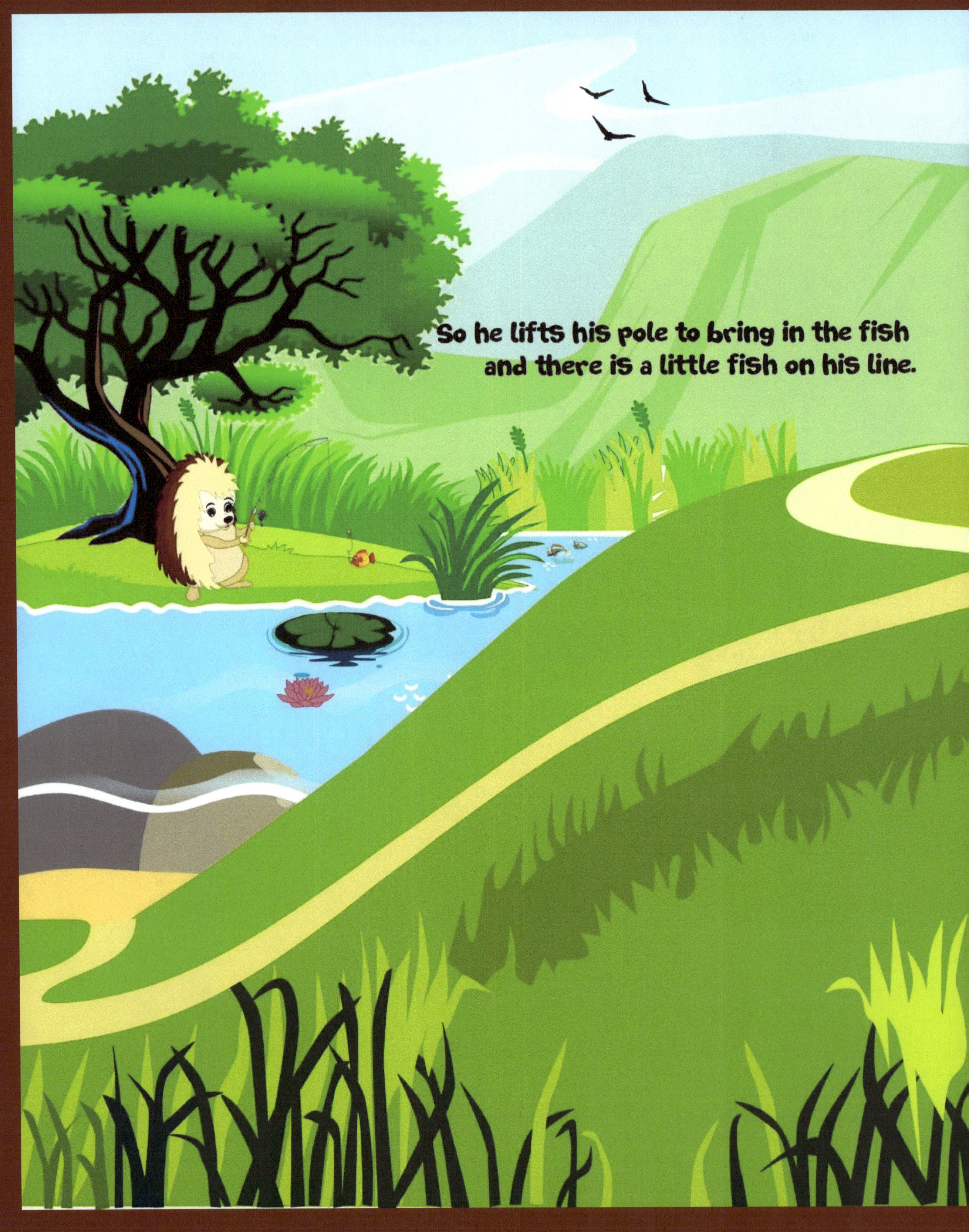

So he lifts his pole to bring in the fish
and there is a little fish on his line.

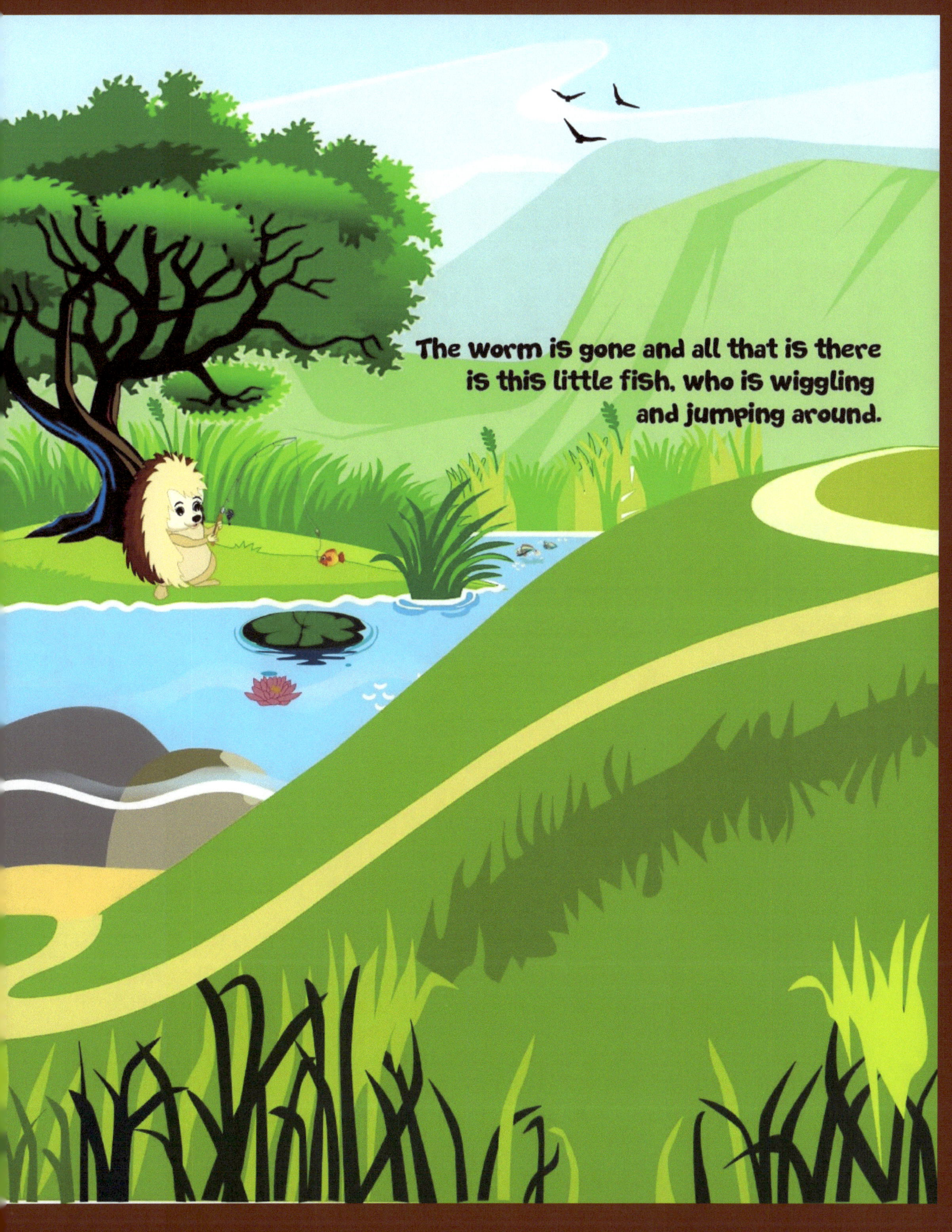
The worm is gone and all that is there
is this little fish, who is wiggling
and jumping around.

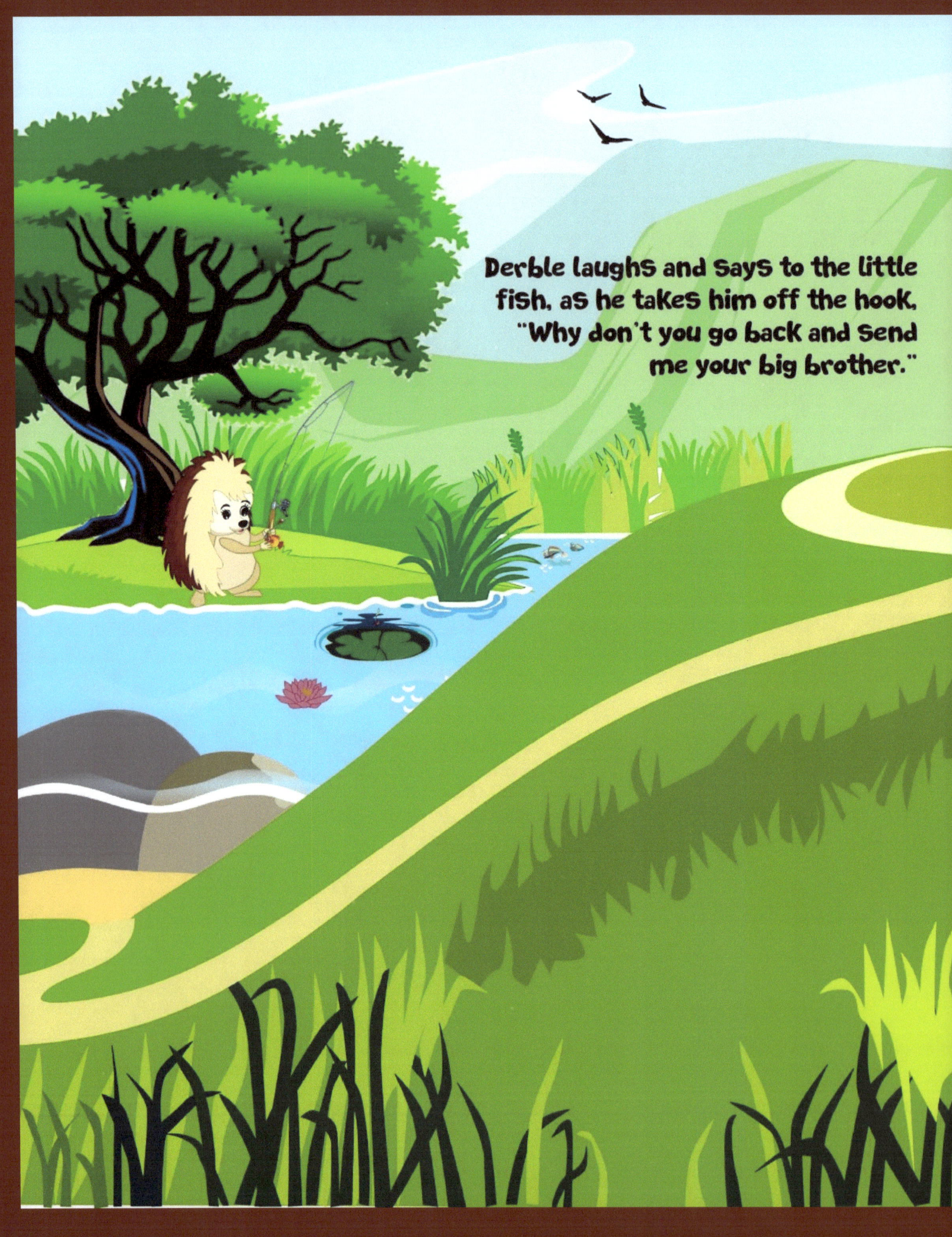

Derble laughs and says to the little fish, as he takes him off the hook, "Why don't you go back and send me your big brother."

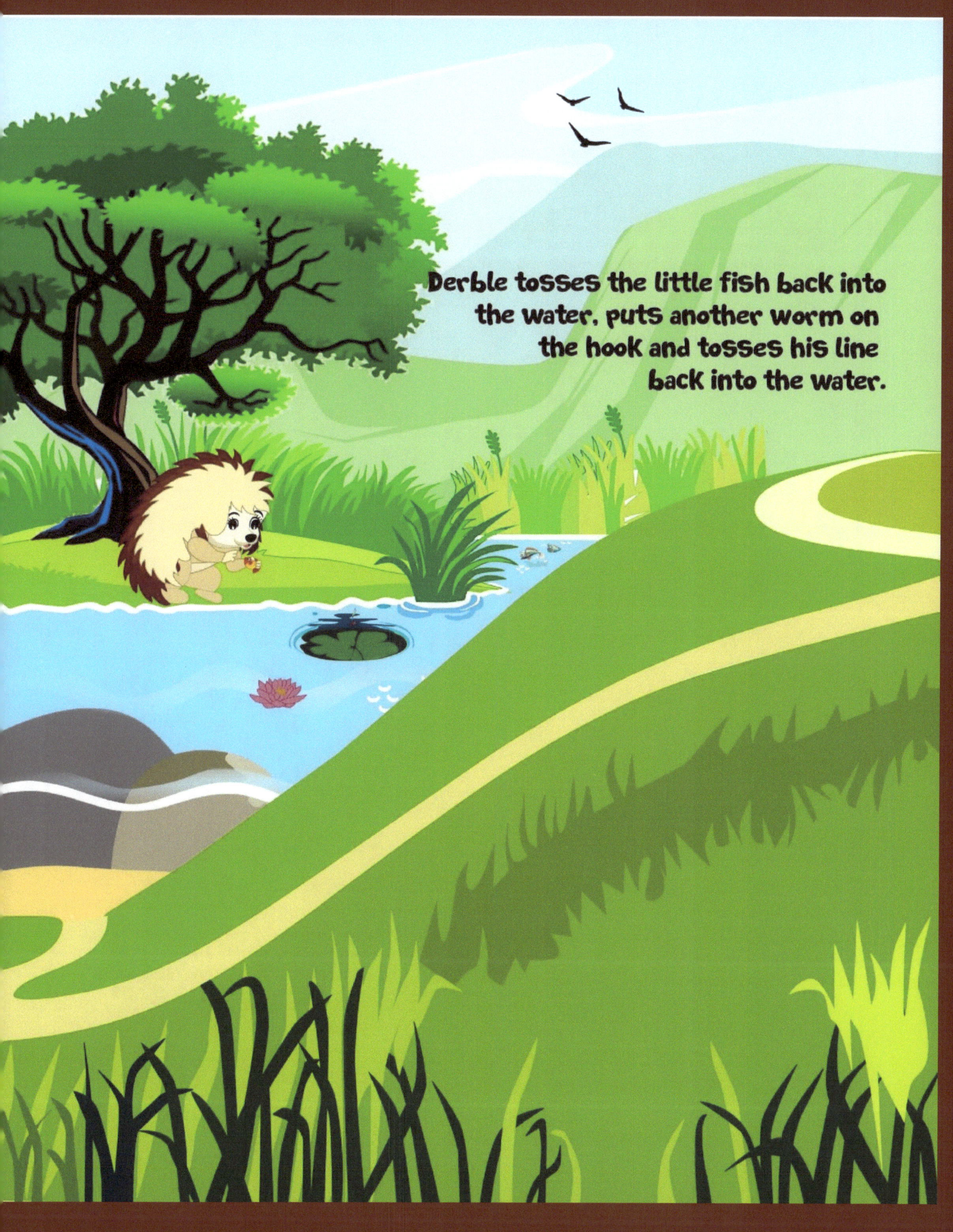
Derble tosses the little fish back into the water, puts another worm on the hook and tosses his line back into the water.

Again, just like before, as soon as the line hits the water, Derble's bobber starts bouncing and going under the water. And again, Derble brings in his line, and again, "it's the same little fish".

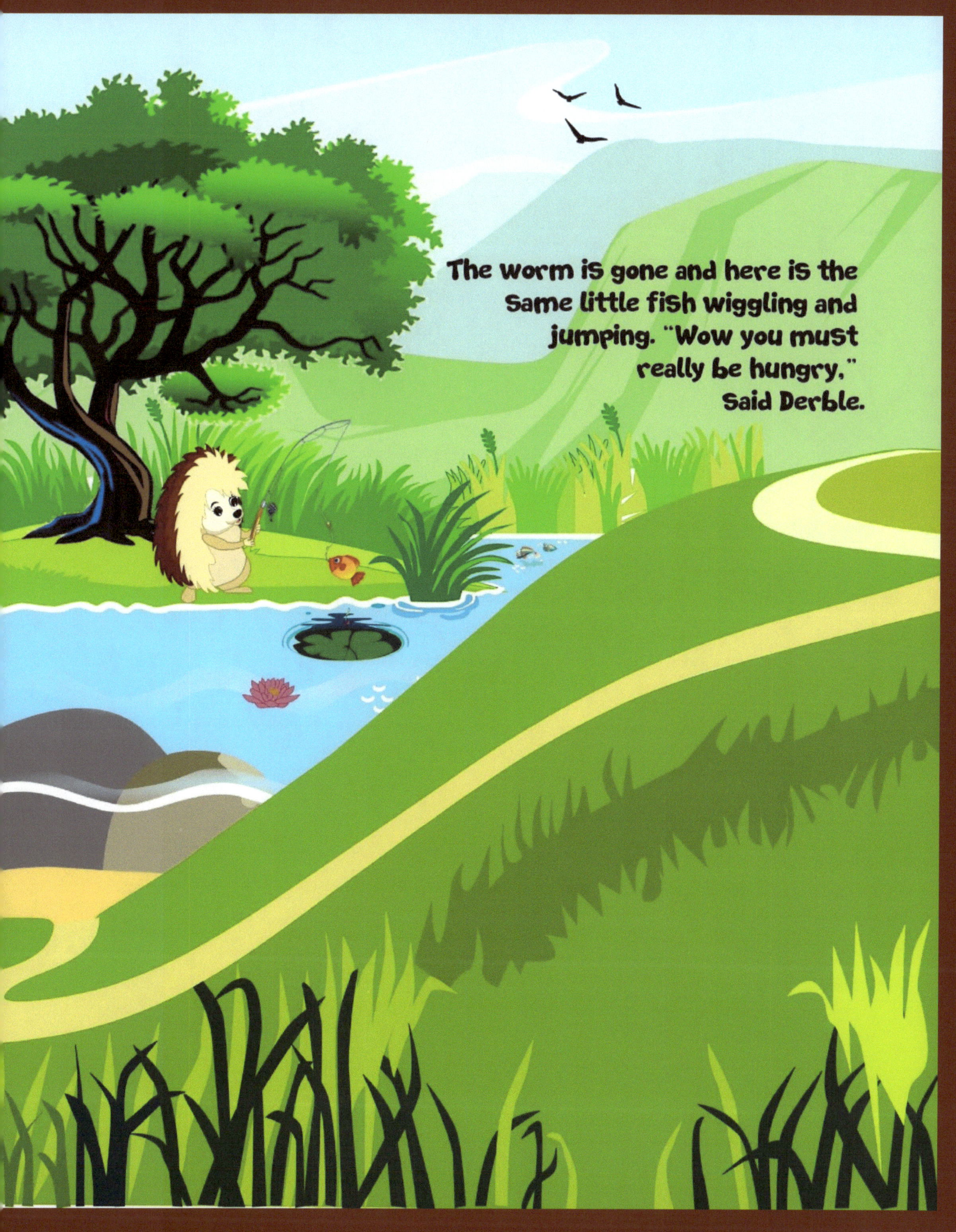
The worm is gone and here is the
Same little fish wiggling and
jumping. "Wow you must
really be hungry,"
Said Derble.

And again, he tells him to send his
big brother as he tosses him back
into the water, the same thing
happens a couple more times,
worm on line, line in water,
bobber bouncing,
same little fish.

So Derble decides it's time to try a
different spot before this little
fish eats up all his worms.

He walks down to the far end of the
pond, puts a worm on his hook,
tosses his line in the water,
and right away his bobber
starts bouncing.

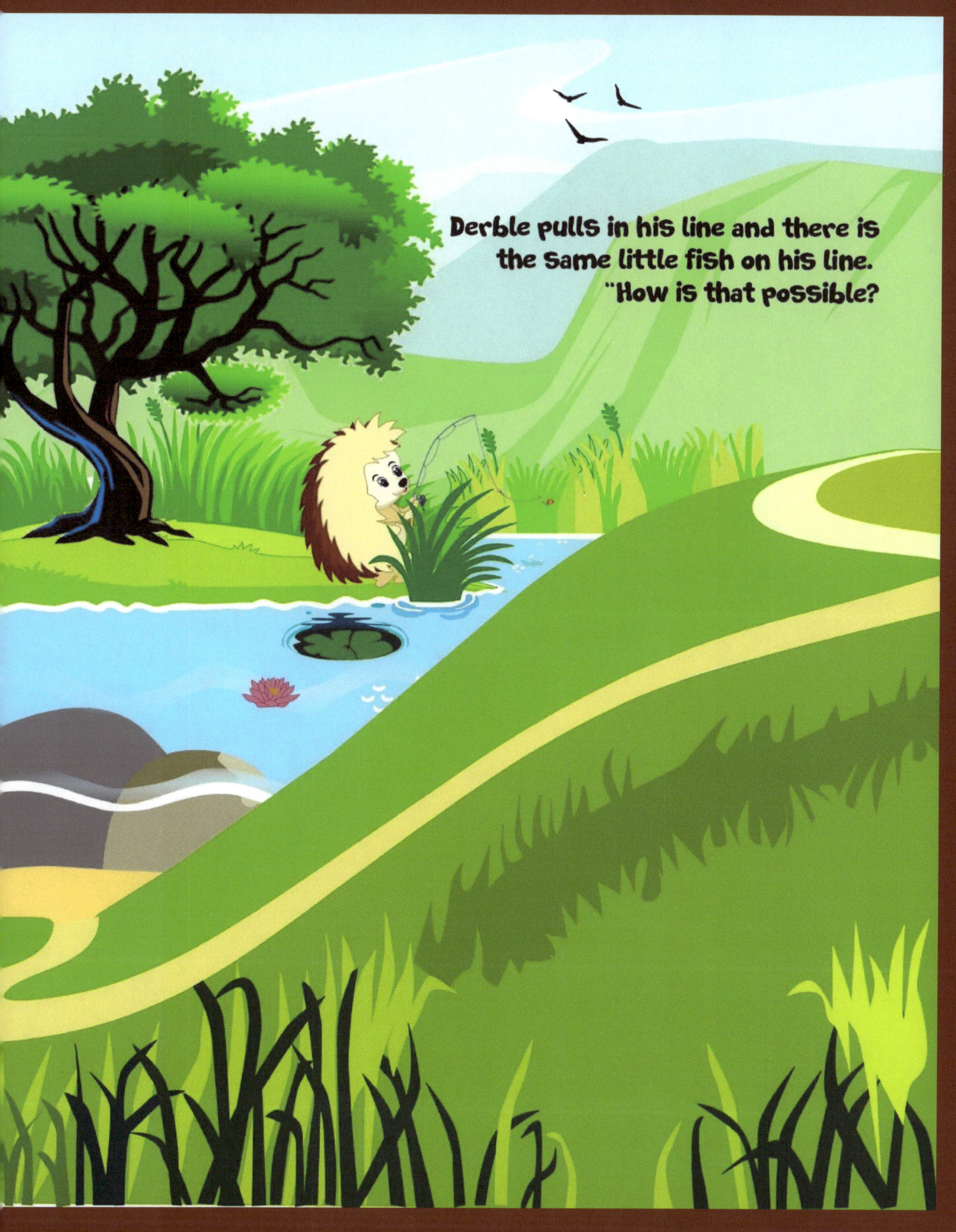

Derble pulls in his line and there is the same little fish on his line. "How is that possible?

He walks down to the far end of the pond, puts a worm on his hook, tosses his line in the water, and right away his bobber starts bouncing.

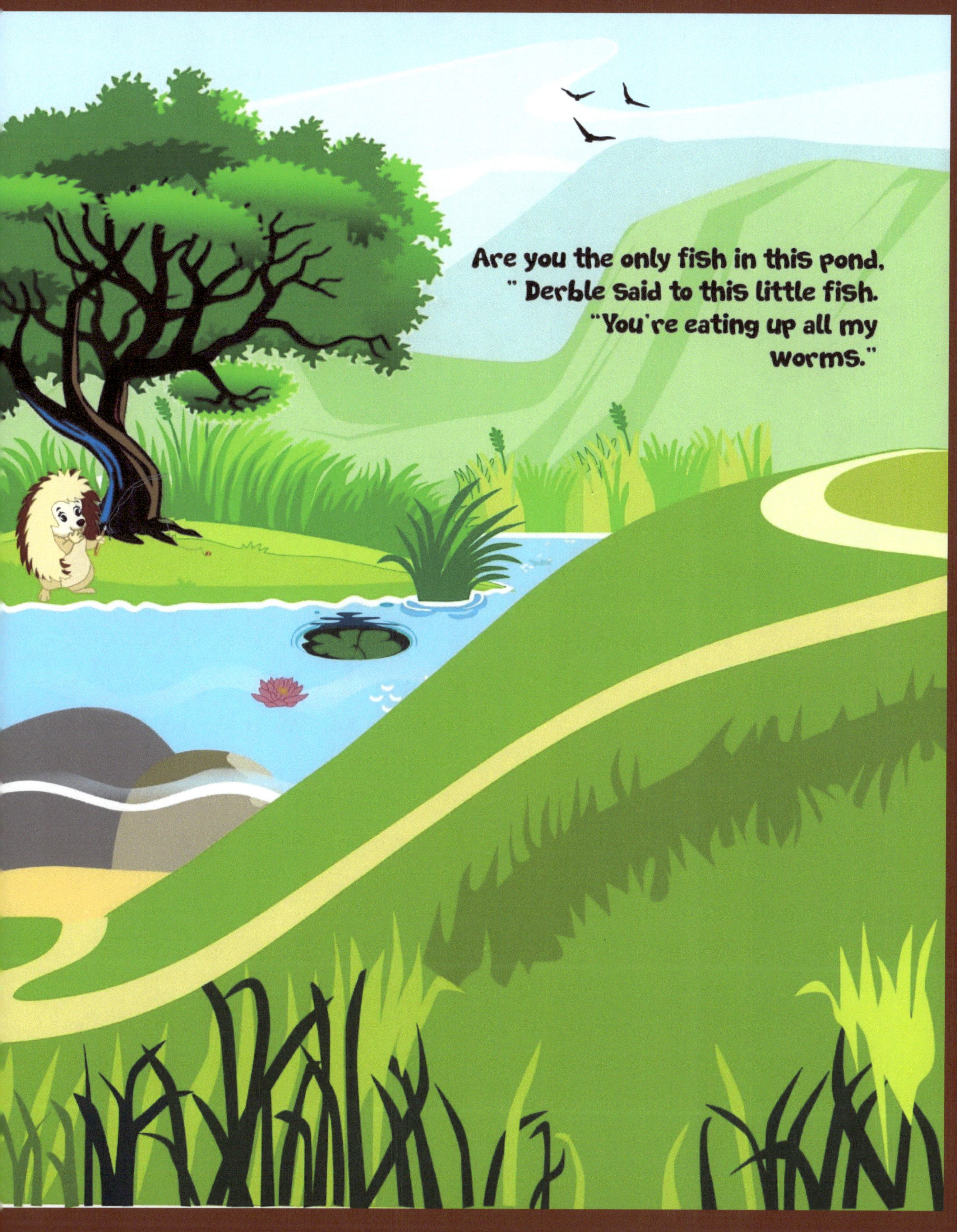

Are you the only fish in this pond,
" Derble said to this little fish.
"You're eating up all my
worms."

So Derble again takes him off his line and tosses him back into the water, and again he moves to a different spot.

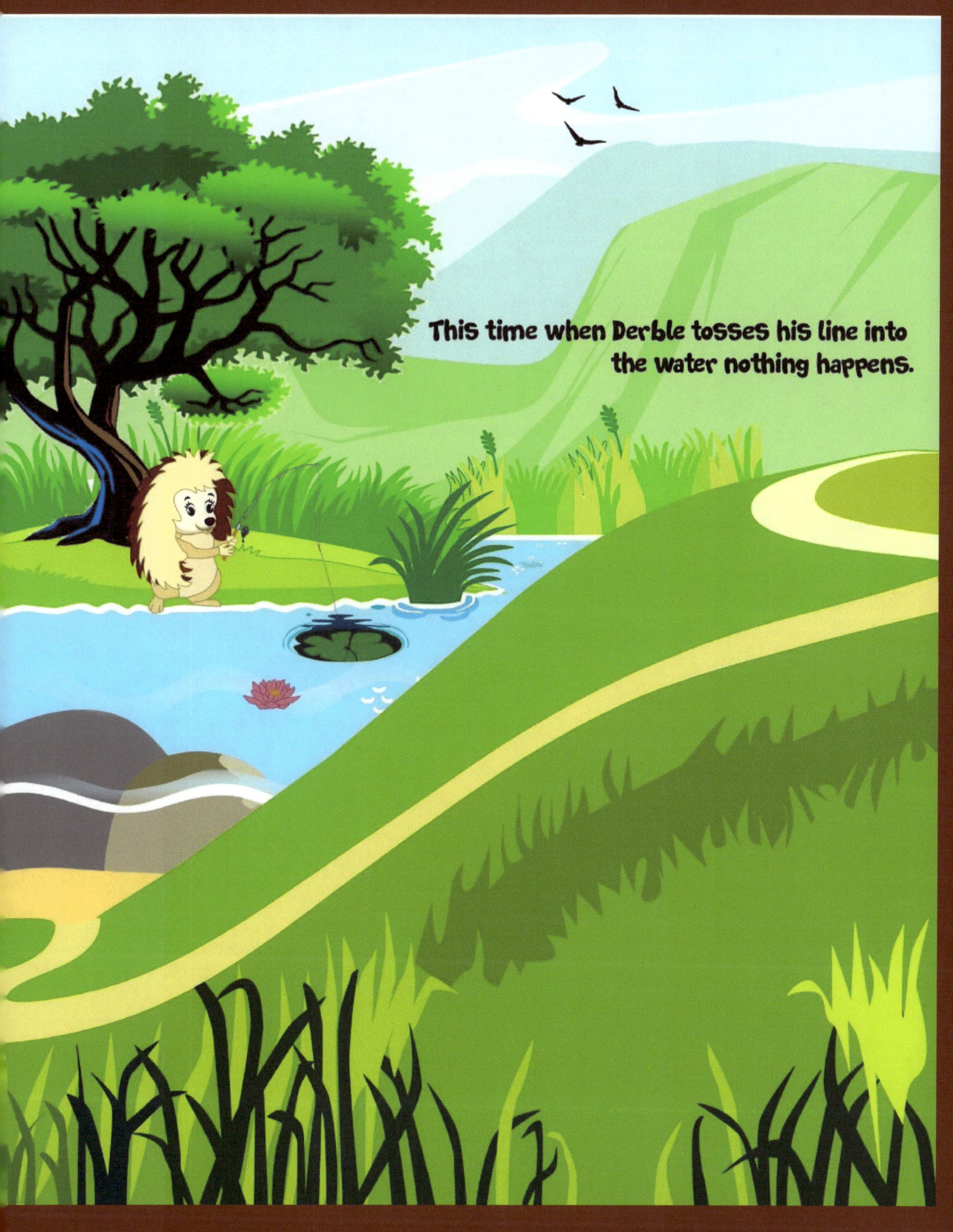
This time when Derble tosses his line into
the water nothing happens.

Not at first, but then after a few minutes, his bobber starts bouncing and when Derble pulls in his line there is the same little fish.

Derble decided to keep the little fish as
his new pet and put him in the pot that
used to hold all of his worms.

He added Some water and the little
fish swam happily around his
new home. Derble decided it
was time to head home.

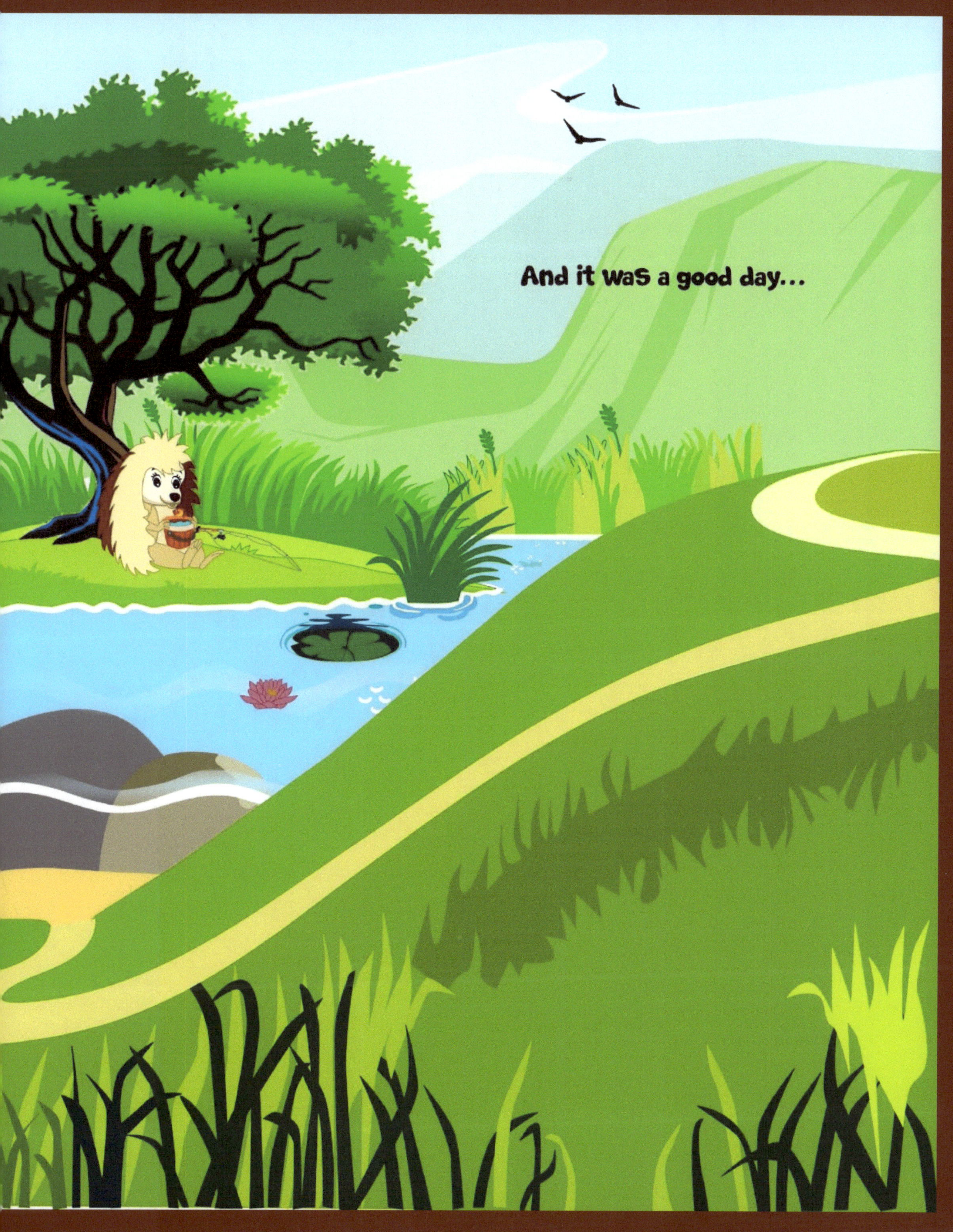
And it was a good day...

www.ingramcontent.com/pod-product-compliance
Lightning Source LLC
Chambersburg PA
CBHW042013110726
48006CB00004B/1071